Luciana: sister of Adriana

Antipholus of Ephesus: son of Egeon and Emilia

Adriana: wife of Antipholus of Ephesus

Dromio of Ephesus: servant of Antipholus of Ephesus

Chapter 1

There was once a merchant called Egeon. He and his wife were on holiday when she gave birth to twin boys. When the first was born, Egeon said, "He looks just like my uncle Antipholus, so I shall name him Antipholus." But a few minutes later, when the second twin was born, he looked exactly the same as his brother. So Egeon named him Antipholus, too.

If that wasn't confusing enough, Egeon had a servant, and the servant's wife also gave birth to twin boys on that very same day. When the first was born, the servant said, "He looks just like my uncle Dromio, so I shall name him Dromio." But a few minutes later, when the second twin was born, he looked exactly the same as his brother. So the servant named him Dromio, too.

So there were two boys named Antipholus who looked exactly the same, and two boys named Dromio who looked exactly the same. Just think of all the confusion that was bound to cause as they were growing up!

Except that it didn't because, at the end of the holiday, they all set off for home in a fine sailing ship ... and their lives were changed forever.

The sea voyage went well for a day or two.

Then a great storm blew up. Huge waves and battering winds tore their ship to pieces. Most of the passengers were washed overboard. Egeon just managed to grab hold of one Antipholus and one Dromio before he too, was swept into the sea. The last he saw of his wife, she was clinging on to the other two babies.

The ship's mast had broken off in the storm.
Egeon tied himself to it, and that kept him and the
babies afloat. Soon afterwards, they were picked up by
a passing fishing boat which took them back to their
home, the city of Syracuse.

Years passed. Antipholus grew up to be a merchant
and Dromio his servant, just like their fathers. They never
forgot their lost brothers, though, and when they were
old enough, they went with Egeon to look for them.
For five years they searched everywhere – except in
the city of Ephesus.

There was a good reason for this: Syracuse and
Ephesus were at war. If anyone from Syracuse was
found in Ephesus, the Duke of Ephesus himself would
throw them into a deep, dark dungeon unless they could
pay a large fine.

But at last, when there was nowhere else left to look, they realised they had to go to Ephesus.

"Let's take enough money to pay the fine," said Egeon. "Just in case."

So the three of them set out for Ephesus. And that's when the trouble *really* started.

Chapter 2

Egeon held on tight to the bag with the money in it for the whole journey. When they arrived in Ephesus, he gave it to Antipholus. "Take this straight to our hotel for safekeeping," he said. "We'll need it if anyone finds out we're from Syracuse!"

"I'm going to have a look around," said Egeon. "I'll see you at the hotel later."

When Antipholus and Dromio had gone, a man came up to Egeon and said, "Did I hear you right? Are you from Syracuse?"

"Yes," whispered Egeon, "but keep your voice down or one of the police officers will hear and I'll be under arrest."

"It's not your lucky day," said the man. "I am one of the police officers, and you are under arrest – unless you can pay the fine by five o'clock this afternoon."

"But they've just taken the bag of money!" said Egeon.

"I know," said the police officer. "Like I say, it's not your lucky day."

Meanwhile, Antipholus and Dromio had reached the marketplace.

"Take the bag of money to our hotel," Antipholus said to Dromio, "and meet me back here."

Dromio took the bag and left. But then he came back almost immediately and said something very odd, which was: "It's time for lunch, master. Your wife is waiting back at the house."

Antipholus took a cucumber from a nearby stall and bopped Dromio on the head with it.

13

"Stop acting the fool!" said Antipholus. "You know perfectly well that I'm not married and I don't live in Ephesus. I come from Syracuse." He said "Syracuse" very quietly so that no one would overhear and arrest him.

Dromio rubbed his sore head for a moment and then he burst out laughing. "You come from Syracuse, master?" he shouted. "Very funny!"

"Stop saying 'Syracuse' you nitwit!" said Antipholus, and he clonked him on the head again. "And where's the bag of money?"

"What bag of money, master?" asked Dromio.

"The bag I just gave you!" Antipholus roared.
He looked like he was going to give Dromio such
a thwack with the cucumber that Dromio ran off.

"I bet he's trying to pinch it!" said Antipholus.
"Everyone knows Ephesus is full of thieves and
swindlers – that must have given him the idea!" And
he went quickly to the hotel to check that the money
was safe.

In fact, Dromio hadn't stolen the bag of money because Antipholus had never given it to him. That was because this was the *other* Dromio: the one Egeon's wife had saved from the shipwreck. He and the other Antipholus had grown up to be a merchant and his servant, just like their brothers, right here in Ephesus.

The other Antipholus, the one living in Ephesus, *was* married. His wife was a beautiful woman called Adriana, and she was waiting for her husband to join her for lunch …

Chapter 3

Adriana, the wife of Antipholus of Ephesus, was sitting with her sister, Luciana, watching their lunch go cold. "There's still no sign of my useless husband, or the useless servant I sent to fetch him," said Adriana.

"At least you've got a husband!" said Luciana sadly. "If I was married, I wouldn't call my husband useless."

"You would if he was anything like mine," said Adriana.

Then Dromio of Ephesus came running into
the house. "The master's gone mad!" he cried. "I found
him in the marketplace but when I said it was time
for lunch, he told me he wasn't married and he comes
from Syracuse!"

"He'll say anything to get out of having lunch
with me!" said Adriana. "Go back and tell him he has
to come."

"And get clonked on the head with a cucumber
again?" said Dromio. "No way!"

"If you don't, I'll clonk you with a rolling pin!"
shouted Adriana.

"Argh!" screamed Dromio, and he ran off again.

"I suppose we'll have to go looking for him ourselves,"
sighed Adriana.

Meanwhile, Antipholus of Syracuse had gone to
the hotel and made sure that the bag of money was safe.
He was just leaving when Dromio of Syracuse bumped
into him in the street outside.

"What are you doing here?" said Dromio. "I thought
you told me to meet you back at the marketplace."

"That's what I thought too," said Antipholus. "But then you started burbling that I never gave you the bag of money in the first place, and that I'm married and my wife wants me to come to lunch!"

He was so cross that he grabbed a plant from a pot by the hotel door and bopped Dromio over the head with it.

"Ouch!" cried Dromio. "No, I didn't!"

This was perfectly true, because of course that was the other Dromio, the one from Ephesus.

But there was no chance that they were going to get that mess sorted out because at that very moment, Adriana and Luciana walked up to them in the street and Adriana said, "Antipholus, my husband! There you are!"

"W-what?" stammered Antipholus. He'd never even seen this woman before and she was calling him her husband!

"Don't you dare pretend you don't know what I'm talking about!" snapped Adriana.

Antipholus didn't know what to say because, of course, he *didn't* know what she was talking about!

"What have I ever done to make you treat me so badly?" said Adriana.

"Nothing!" said Antipholus. "I've only just arrived in Ephesus! I've never seen you before in my life!"

"How can you be so horrible to my sister?"
said Luciana. "She sent Dromio to get you."

"But she didn't send me!" said Dromio.

Antipholus looked at Dromio. He started to wonder if
everyone had gone a bit mad. "That was when you were
burbling on about me being married and having to come
home to lunch! And don't say it wasn't you because how
else would this lady know your name?"

"Never mind all that!" said Adriana, grabbing hold of Antipholus. "You're coming home with me now!"

"What's going on, master?" asked Dromio.

"I don't know!" said Antipholus. "But maybe we should just go with them to lunch."

Chapter 4

Meanwhile, the other Antipholus, the one who had been brought up in Ephesus, and who actually *was* married to Adriana, was at a jeweller's shop. This Antipholus was having a necklace made for Adriana as a surprise present.

"Shall I bring it over to your house when it's finished?" asked the jeweller.

"Oh yes, you'd better," said Antipholus, looking at the time. "I'm already late for lunch and Adriana doesn't like that."

Antipholus had almost reached his house when he bumped into Dromio – his Dromio, the one from Ephesus. "Has my wife sent you to fetch me for lunch?" Antipholus asked.

"Argh!" cried Dromio. "Please don't bop me on the head with a cucumber again!"

"A cucumber?!" said Antipholus. "What are you talking about?"

But when they got back to Antipholus's house, things only got stranger.

The door was locked for a start.

"What's she done that for?" Antipholus wondered. He knocked on the door.

"Go away!" said a voice from the other side of the door.

"I beg your pardon!" said Antipholus. "I've come for my lunch!"

"Don't care," said the voice.

"Let me have a go," said Dromio, and he knocked on the door. "Who is it that dares keep my master out of his own house?"

"I'm Dromio," said the voice.

"What?!" cried Dromio.

Here's what had happened. A few minutes earlier, the other Antipholus and Dromio – the ones from Syracuse – had arrived at the house with Adriana and Luciana. Adriana had ordered Dromio to lock the door and not let anyone in. She was so cross with Antipholus that she didn't want anyone to disturb them while she gave him a good telling off.

"Open this door!" yelled the other Antipholus from outside. He banged so loudly on the door that Adriana heard and came to see what all the fuss was about.

"The people in this town are a bit rowdy, mistress," said Dromio.

"Is that my wife in there?" cried Antipholus from outside.

"I'm no wife of yours!" Adriana shouted back. "Go away!"

"That's the spirit!" said Dromio of Syracuse. "Tell him to get lost!"

By now, Antipholus was furious. "If they won't let us in, we'll break in!" he snarled.

But Dromio of Ephesus stopped him. "I'm sure it's just a misunderstanding, master," he said. "It's not worth getting angry about. Let's go and have lunch somewhere else."

"I'll go all right!" grumbled Antipholus. "But I'll be back!"

Chapter 5

While all this was going on, the other Antipholus
– the one from Syracuse – was inside the house
with Luciana. They were in the dining room, which was
so far away from the front door that they hadn't heard
any of the shouting and banging. Besides, they had
other things on their minds.

"You're being mean to my sister," said Luciana. "She
loves you very much and you keep pretending that
you don't know who she is. You might be a bit fed up
with her but that doesn't matter. You should still treat
her kindly."

"Beautiful lady," said Antipholus, gazing into
Luciana's eyes. "I don't know your name, but whatever
you want me to do, I will, because I'm in love with you."

"Me?" said Luciana. "No, you're in love with my sister!"

"I'm in love with your sister's sister," said Antipholus dreamily.

"But that's me, too!" said Luciana. "Oh no, what a mess!"

"No it's not," said Antipholus. "You're not married, I'm not married. It's perfect!"

"But you *are* married!" said Luciana.

Antipholus was so love-struck he wasn't listening; he just stared adoringly into Luciana's eyes.

Unsure what to say next, Luciana jumped up and ran off.

No sooner had Luciana ran out of the room than Dromio of Syracuse ran in.

"You'll never guess what's happened now!" he said. "There's a man banging on the door saying this is his house and he wants his lunch! He sounded quite cross."

"There's something very strange going on here," said Antipholus. "Adriana says she's my wife, even though I've never seen her before and Luciana is so beautiful, I feel like she's cast a spell on me. We've got to get out of here or we'll go crazy. I'll sneak out of the house without either of them noticing. You go to the docks and find us a ship to sail away on."

31

Antipholus made sure no one
saw him as he slipped out of
the house. He'd only gone a few
steps, though, when he felt
a tap on the shoulder. "Argh!"
he cried and whirled round. It was
the jeweller.

"I've finished your necklace,"
said the jeweller.

"What necklace?" asked
Antipholus, because, of course, it was the other
Antipholus who'd ordered it.

"This one here," said the jeweller, bringing out
the most beautiful – and expensive – necklace Antipholus
had ever seen. "You're Antipholus, aren't you?"

"Yes," said Antipholus.

"Then this is your necklace," said the jeweller, and he
gave it to him.

"Don't you want some money for it?"
asked Antipholus.

"You can pay me later today," said the jeweller.

"But what if I just take it and don't pay you?"
asked Antipholus.

"Good joke!" chuckled the jeweller and he walked off.

"What an odd place this is!" muttered Antipholus, as he fastened the necklace around his neck for safekeeping. "People just give you expensive necklaces in the street!"

The jeweller was still chuckling when he got back to his shop. A merchant was waiting there for him.

"You remember that money I lent you?" said the merchant. "Well I'd like it back now, please."

"Of course," said the jeweller. "As a matter of fact, Antipholus owes me the same amount of money for a necklace I've just given him. And look, here he comes!"

33

But this was the other Antipholus, Antipholus of Ephesus, so when the jeweller asked him for the money for the necklace, this Antipholus said, quite rightly, "But you didn't give me the necklace!"

"Is this another joke?" said the jeweller. "Come on, pay up."

"How many times? You didn't give me the necklace!" said Antipholus.

"Then who did I give it to?" said the jeweller.

"I don't know!" snapped Antipholus.

The merchant could see that he wasn't going to get his money so he called a police officer over.

"You've always been a good customer," said the jeweller. "I don't want to ask this police officer to arrest you."

"For the last time, you didn't give me the necklace!" said Antipholus.

The jeweller didn't mind his customers making jokes, but he got very cross if anyone called him a liar. He told the police officer to handcuff Antipholus at once.

"You'll regret this!" said Antipholus. "When I'm proved innocent, no one will ever trust you or come to this shop again!"

And then Dromio appeared. Only this was Dromio
of Syracuse.

"Master," he said, "I've done what you asked. I've got
us a ship to sail away on!"

"So you were going to cheat me!" cried the jeweller.
"You were going to run away with my necklace!
I knew it!"

Antipholus sighed. It just wasn't his lucky day.
"I need money or I'm going to prison," he said.
"Go and get some from Adriana!"

"Adriana?" asked Dromio. "Why should she give
you money?"

"Just ask her!" cried Antipholus. "Quickly!"

Chapter 6

Back at the house, Luciana was telling Adriana what Antipholus of Syracuse had said. "He swore over and over again that he wasn't married to you," she said.

Angry tears welled up in Adriana's eyes and Luciana put her arms around her.

"The really funny thing is," Luciana went on, "if I didn't know better, I could have sworn he was telling the truth," and she took a deep breath, "even when he said he was in love with me instead."

"That wretch!" said Adriana. "How could he?"

"There must be something wrong with him," said Luciana.

Before she could say more, Dromio came rushing into the house.

"What's the matter?" asked Luciana.

"Antipholus has been arrested!" said Dromio.

"What for?" asked Adriana.

"Some nonsense about a necklace," said Dromio. "He needs money or he'll go to prison. I told him you wouldn't give it to him."

Adriana took a deep breath. "Despite everything, he's still my husband," she said, and she gave Dromio a purse of money. "Go and set him free."

The other Antipholus, the one from Syracuse who did have the necklace, walked through the streets of Ephesus in wonder. Wherever he went, people knew his name, they invited him in for tea and they even offered him money!

So when Dromio ran up and gave him the purse of money from Adriana, this Antipholus said, "Not you too!"

"Where's the police officer gone?" asked Dromio.

"What police officer?" said Antipholus.

"The one who arrested you, of course!" said Dromio.

"Stop talking nonsense!" snapped Antipholus. "Did you find us a ship to sail away on?"

"I told you that before!" said Dromio. "When the police officer was arresting you!"

"You must be seeing things!" cried Antipholus.

Meanwhile, Antipholus of Ephesus was on his way to prison. "My wife's in a strange mood today," he said to the police officer who was taking him there. "I wouldn't like to be in your shoes when she finds out what you've done. Just you wait till my servant comes back with the money."

At that moment, Dromio came back empty-handed.

"Where's the money?" asked Antipholus.

"What money?" asked Dromio – because this was the *other* Dromio, the one from Ephesus. "You didn't say anything about any money."

Antipholus was so angry he tried to attack Dromio.

"Calm down!" said the police officer. "There are ladies approaching."

It was Adriana and Luciana.

"Right you two," said Antipholus. "I've had enough of your mucking about for one day."

Adriana took one look at Antipholus and said, "You're right, Luciana. There is something wrong with him."

"There's nothing wrong with me!" roared Antipholus.

"Then what are you so angry about?" asked Adriana.

"You locked me out of my own house for one thing!" said Antipholus, and Dromio agreed.

Luciana couldn't believe her ears. "You had lunch with us!" she said.

Antipholus thought they must be playing a huge joke on him. "I bet you even paid the jeweller to get me arrested, you wicked women!" he said.

"I sent Dromio with a purse of money to set you free!" Adriana replied, and Luciana agreed.

"No you didn't!" said Dromio.

Antipholus was so upset he started to cry. "Will somebody please start telling the truth?" he sobbed. He looked so miserable, Adriana took pity on him.

"Set him free, officer," she said. "I'll pay the jeweller what he owes. Dromio, take Antipholus back to the house and lock him in so he can't do himself any harm. We'll go and find a doctor to take care of him."

"Come on, master," said Dromio, dragging Antipholus away.

"But there's nothing wrong with me!" screamed Antipholus furiously as Adriana and Luciana walked off. "Why doesn't anyone believe me?"

Chapter 7

The other Antipholus and Dromio couldn't wait to get out of Ephesus. They were on their way to their hotel to find Egeon – who, they thought, would be waiting for them there – when they passed the jeweller.

"How did you escape from the police officer?" asked the jeweller. "He was taking you to prison!"

"Run, Dromio!" cried Antipholus. He'd no idea what the jeweller was on about, but he certainly didn't want to go to prison.

"And you *have* got my necklace, you fibber! You're wearing it!" cried the jeweller as they ran off. "Police! Stop them!"

A group of police officers heard the jeweller's cries and went after Antipholus and Dromio.

Antipholus and Dromio ran into a little square where they nearly bumped into ... Adriana and Luciana.

"Argh!" cried Antipholus and Dromio.

"Argh!" cried Adriana and Luciana.

Police officers poured into the square.

"We're surrounded, master," said Dromio. "What are we going to do?"

Antipholus looked around wildly and then he saw it: they were standing outside an abbey! "The nuns will take care of us!" he cried. "Inside! Quickly!"

They ran straight up to the abbess and fell on the ground in front of her.

"Please help us!" Antipholus begged. "We haven't done anything wrong, but all these people are chasing us!"

The abbess, a kindly old lady called Emilia, said, "Don't worry. I'll speak to them."

She stepped out into the square, but before she could say anything, the abbey clock struck five. At once, there was a fanfare of trumpets. The Duke of Ephesus himself came riding grandly by. Behind him, guards dragged Egeon, looking very sorry for himself. No one had paid his fine so it was time for the duke to throw him into the deep, dark dungeon.

Adriana knelt before the duke, and he stopped.

"My husband is hiding in that abbey, sir," she said. "Please ask him to come out. He'll listen to you."

At that moment, one of Adriana's servants came rushing into the square. "Antipholus has escaped from the doctor at your house, and Dromio's chasing him!" he cried.

"But they never got to my house!" said Adriana. "They're in this abbey here, as I've just told the duke!"

As if to prove her wrong, Antipholus and Dromio ran into the square from the other direction.

"There you are, great duke!" cried Antipholus. "I beg you help us! My wife has been playing cruel tricks on me all day long and I can't stand it any more!"

"How can he be out here and in the abbey at the same time?!" cried Adriana. "I don't understand!"

"Lunch!" shrieked Antipholus. "Locked doors! Jewellers! Necklace! Money! It's enough to drive anyone round the bend!"

"Wait a moment!" said Egeon. "I know that young man! It's my son!"

Chapter 8

"But I don't remember my father!" said Antipholus. "He was lost in a shipwreck when I was a baby."

"That's a coincidence!" said the abbess. "A long time ago, I rescued two babies from a shipwreck."

Before Egeon could say anything, the other Antipholus and Dromio came out of the abbey.

"W-w-what?" stammered Adriana, looking at both Antipholuses. "Have I got two husbands?"

51

"I only ever had one," said the abbess, "and for years I thought I'd lost him in that same shipwreck, but there he is! Egeon, my love!"

"Emilia! My wife! Is it really you?" cried Egeon, and they ran into one another's arms.

"I'm beginning to understand what's been going on here," said Antipholus of Ephesus. "All along, you thought I was him ..."

"... and you were me!" said Antipholus of Syracuse. "Then this necklace is yours."

"It belongs to my beloved wife," said Antipholus of Ephesus, and he hung it around Adriana's neck and kissed her.

"Brother!" cried the Antipholuses and they embraced.

"Brother!" cried the Dromios and they embraced, too.

"So *that* Antipholus has been a good husband to you all along," said Luciana to her sister, "and *this* Antipholus was telling the truth when he said he wasn't married ..."

"... and that I love you!" said Antipholus of Syracuse, and he gathered Luciana up in his arms.

"So your family has been reunited after all this time!" said the duke. "Love is in the air and there's a wedding in the offing! This is wonderful news! Set Egeon free!"

Everyone cheered and they all went into the abbey to celebrate.

"Well I didn't see that coming," said Dromio of Ephesus. "Not after a day like today!"

"You know what they say, brother," said Dromio of Syracuse. "All's well that ends well!"

Twins in a spin!

Downtown Ephesus ground to a halt yesterday.
Abbey Square was closed to traffic, causing a long tailback of carts and donkeys. The chaos was caused by a police chase sparked by two sets of long-lost twins.

"I thought I was seeing double," says glamorous Adriana. "My husband seemed to have gone mad. I had him dragged away and seen by a doctor. Imagine my surprise when, a few moments later, he came running out of the abbey!"

"I knew my master wasn't himself," confirms loyal servant, Dromio. "He kept clonking me on the head with a cucumber!"

The man in question is Antipholus, a young merchant. He and his twin brother, also Antipholus, and their servants, Dromio and his twin brother (also Dromio)

were separated as babies in a shipwreck many years ago. But Antipholus of Syracuse never gave up looking for his brother and travelled to Ephesus to find him. The twins then spent most of yesterday being mistaken for one another.

"I've never seen anything like it," says the police officer. "Two men looking like one another – twice! There should be a law against it!"

All four twins were finally reunited by his grace, the Duke of Ephesus, who was quoted as saying, "In the end, it was much ado about nothing."

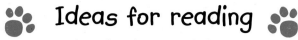

Ideas for reading

Written by Clare Dowdall, PhD
Lecturer and Primary Literacy Consultant

Reading objectives:
- identify and discuss themes and conventions in and across a wide range of writing
- prepare poems and plays to read aloud and to perform, showing understanding through intonation, tone and volume so that the meaning is clear to an audience
- summarise the main ideas drawn from more than one paragraph, identifying key details that support the main ideas

Spoken language objectives:
- participate in discussions, presentations, performances, role play, improvisations and debates
- select and use appropriate registers for effective communication

Curriculum links: PSHE – relationships (special people)

Resources: paper and pencils; digital camera; photographs and drawings of "special people"

Build a context for reading
- Introduce the book and explain that this is a famous comedy by William Shakespeare.
- Discuss what the words "comedy" and "error" mean. Ask children to suggest examples of funny errors that they've made to create a shared understanding of the meaning of these words.
- Read the blurb to the children. Discuss what's special about identical twins.

Understand and apply reading strategies
- Turn to pp2–3. Read the characters' names and descriptions with the children and sketch a rough diagram to show how they're connected (a family tree).